Haffertee Goes to Hospital

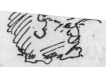

Copyright © 1993 Janet and John Perkins
Illustrations copyright © 1993 Diane Matthes

The authors assert the moral right to be identified as the
authors of this work.

The
Diamond
Family

Fran   Ma

Diamond Lo
with
Hafferkee and
Howl Out

Pops

Mark

Chris.

Copyright © 1993 Janet and John Perkins
Illustrations copyright © 1993 Diane Matthes

The authors assert the moral right to be identified as the
authors of this work.

Published by
Lion Publishing plc
Sandy Lane West, Oxford, England
ISBN 0 7459 2401 8
Albatross Books Pty Ltd
PO Box 320, Sutherland, NSW 2232, Australia
ISBN 0 7324 0588 2

First edition 1993

A catalogue record for this book
is available from the British Library

Printed and bound in Great Britain by
BPCC Hazells Ltd
Member of BPCC Ltd

Haffertee Goes to Hospital

Haffertee is a toy hamster. Ma
Diamond made him for her little girl,
Yolanda (usually known as Yo), when
her pet hamster died.

In this book—the seventh in the
series—Haffertee takes care of Yo in
hospital after she falls off her bike. He
meets Mr X Ray and Yo's leg gets put
in plaster. Haffertee also learns about
the wonderful way our bodies are made,
and how sick people can get better.

The charm of the stories lies in the
funny, lovable character of Haffertee
himself, and in the special place God
has in the affections of Yo and her
family.

The Diamond Family

Frau   Ma

Diamond Lo
with
Haffertee and
Howl Out

Pops

Mark

Chris.

Haffertee

Goes to Hospital

Janet and John Perkins

A LION PAPERBACK

Oxford · Batavia · Sydney

Published by
Lion Publishing plc
Sandy Lane West, Oxford, England
ISBN 0 7459 2401 8
Albatross Books Pty Ltd
PO Box 320, Sutherland, NSW 2232, Australia
ISBN 0 7324 0588 2

First edition 1993

A catalogue record for this book
is available from the British Library

Printed and bound in Great Britain by
BPCC Hazells Ltd

Member of BPCC Ltd

Contents

1

Diamond Yo is Broken

It was Diamond Yo's birthday and Haffertee was up early. Diamond Yo was still getting dressed. Pops Diamond called him out into the front garden.

"I've got something to show you," he whispered.

"Wowee!" shouted Haffertee, jumping up and down. "What a bike!"

It was beautiful. Red and white and shining.

Pops Diamond smiled. "D'you think she'll like it?"

Haffertee gasped. "Like it?" he said. "She'll love it!"

He was right. Yo loved it as soon as she saw it. It was just what she wanted.

A brand new bicycle on her birthday. Standing there against the garage door and waiting to be ridden.

She hopped up and down with delight.

"Many Returns of this Happy Day," spluttered Haffertee. "What a lovely bike!" He winked at Howl Owl, who was sitting on the garden fence.

Howl Owl was Haffertee's very special friend. He was a big, soft, huggable, round, brown owl.

Yo was busy showing Fran, her older sister, the pedals and the handlebars and the saddle and the tyres and the... just everything.

"Only a short ride, Yo," said Pops. "Then you must come in for breakfast or you'll be late for school."

Fran helped her steer the new bike down the steep front drive and on to the path below Hillside House.

"Come on, Haffertee," Yo called eagerly. "This basket in front is just right for you. Jump in. Hold tight."

Haffertee jumped in and held tight. He could see out of the basket through the wire mesh. What a way to travel!

Yo checked that he was safe and then sat herself firmly on the saddle. It was easy.

They glided off along the pavement, slowly, slowly.

It was a quiet lane and the pavement was hardly ever used.

The rest of the family watched from inside the house.

Ma Diamond and Grandma were a bit frightened because it was the first time Yo had ridden a bike that size.

"She will stay on the pavement," said Pops firmly.

As they came back past Hillside House Haffertee waved to Fran on the drive, Howl on the fence and the others at the window. Yo began to sing . . .

Out on my bike
Pedalling along
Nobody here in my way.
Out in the sun
Singing a song
This is my Birthday today.

She felt very happy. So did Haffertee.

Then suddenly, when everything seemed just right, Mrs Ellington Purrswell, the Diamond family cat, ran out in front of them. The spotted dog from up the road was chasing her.

Yo swerved sharply, all at once.

Crunch! Right into Miss Moreton's low wall.

Haffertee was thrown out of the basket and flew gracefully over into Miss Moreton's flower bed.

He stood up straight away, brushed some petals and leaves off his head and looked round to see where he was. He moved himself very carefully and was delighted to discover he was all together.

Diamond Yo wasn't.

As Haffertee climbed back over the wall he saw her lying on the pavement crumpled and still.

There was blood around her elbow.

The bicycle had fallen on its side and the back wheel was spinning.

Howl Owl fluttered down onto the wall.

Big sister Fran came and knelt beside Yo and talked to her calmly.

Pops, Ma and Yo's big brothers, Chris and Mark, came running.

They stood there looking down at her.

She moaned softly, moved her head slowly and opened her eyes. She tried to turn and couldn't.

"Oh! My leg!" she cried. "My leg!"

The tears came. Haffertee snuggled into her neck and tried to catch them in his fur.

Pops knelt down beside Fran and looked at a strange bend in Yo's leg. He nodded to Ma Diamond and she went quickly back to the house. She was going to phone for an ambulance and to tell Grandma what had happened.

Mark fetched a pillow for Yo's head and a blanket to cover her.

"We mustn't let you move, Yo," said Pops, "because we don't quite know what's the matter. We'll wait for the ambulance."

"Would you like a drink of water, Yo?" said Haffertee gently.

"Better not, Haffertee," said Pops kindly. "She hasn't had anything yet this morning. I think we'll keep it that way."

Yo sighed and cried and waited. It was not a

very nice way to spend a birthday.

Haffertee stayed snuggled close, his own tears overflowing onto his cheeks. Diamond Yo was hurting and there was nothing he could do.

He looked at Fran. She was talking quietly to someone.

"Who are you talking to?" asked Haffertee, with a sob.

"To God," said Fran. "That's the best thing I can do now."

"Can he mend Yo?" asked Haffertee, more cheerfully.

Fran smiled and nodded. "Yes, he can," she said. "You just wait and see."

Haffertee looked at Howl Owl sitting on the wall and the two of them nodded. They were going to wait and see together.

2

Ambulance Ride

Haffertee knew that Yo was hurting badly. She had fallen off her bike before and had got up straight away. But this time she was lying so still under the blanket. She had stopped crying but her face was white.

Haffertee looked at the bike. The front wheel was bent and the handlebars were crooked.

Some of the lovely red paint had been scratched off and the basket in front was only just hanging on.

Mrs Ellington Purrswell was wandering up and down. She was so cross with herself for running in front of Yo and causing the accident.

The spotted dog wasn't far away. He lay with his head on his front paws looking very sad.

Before long the ambulance arrived.

Haffertee sighed.

The rest of the family cheered.

"Thank you, God," whispered Pops.

"Yes, thank you," said Ma.

Haffertee knew they had both been praying that it would come quickly.

Two men in smart uniforms got out.

"Hello!" said the driver, "What's happened here?"

They walked over to see Yo crumpled on the ground.

Pops explained what had happened.

One of the men took off the blanket slowly.

"I'll get out of your way," squeaked Haffertee

and scrambled on to the low wall to sit next to Howl.

"Thank you," said the man, and began to examine Yo.

He was very careful.

"Ummmm!" he said at last. "Your left elbow hurts, doesn't it, Yo? And that leg looks very painful. We will soon get you to hospital."

He went to the back of the ambulance and opened the doors.

Some steps folded down out of the back of the ambulance and settled firmly on the road.

"Here comes a long bed for you, Yo," shouted Haffertee, jumping down from the wall.

The men put the stretcher down beside her.

Yo held Haffertee firmly in her right hand.

The two men began to move her very carefully on to the stretcher.

Yo was very brave. She just squeezed Haffertee a little, but she didn't cry.

She was finally settled and Haffertee snuggled in around her neck again.

Yo tickled his whiskers and poggled his ears.

"Haffertee," she whispered. "Haffertee. Thank you for coming."

Haffertee felt great.

He was with Yo just when she needed him.

That was the very best place to be.

The men lifted both of them up into the ambulance.

"Here's your bag," said Pops, handing it to Ma. "We've put your nighties and tooth-brushes in there. Give us a ring as soon as you can and we'll all come in and see how things are. We can bring anything else then."

"Thanks," said Ma, and gave them all a hug.

Holding the bag, she got into the ambulance and sat down on a seat opposite Yo.

Howl Owl flew in and perched next to her.

One of the men got in and locked the back doors.

He turned and began to make sure Yo was comfortable.

Haffertee thought he had a kind face and whispered it to Yo.

The man smiled. "Thank you," he said, "we do our best."

Another door shut, the engine started up and away they went.

Haffertee could feel the ambulance swerving and twisting as it rushed Yo to the hospital.

"Won't be long now," said the man, as he sat down next to Ma Diamond. "Steve is a good driver."

Ma Diamond nodded. "I'm glad to hear it,"

she said. "The traffic in town is often very bad."

Haffertee stood up on the pillow.

The ambulance was slowing down.

"So many cars," he said, looking out of the window.

Ma Diamond began to bite her lower lip.

Slower and slower... and slower... and almost stopped.

"Don't worry," said the ambulance man, "Steve'll soon fix that."

Even as he spoke the weird sound began.

...EEEEEEE...AAAAAAAWWWWW... EEEEEEE...AAAAAAAWWWWW...!!!!

Yo jumped and then settled again.

Haffertee shuddered and hid under Yo's blanket.

"That's the ambulance siren," shouted the man. "We use it to help us get through the traffic."

Haffertee covered his ears. What a noise!

The ambulance began to move faster.

"Won't be long now," said the ambulance man again.

"You just wait and see."

Once more Haffertee decided to do just that.

3
Looking at Yo

As soon as the ambulance arrived in the hospital yard the doors were opened. Haffertee and Yo were settled on a trolley and wheeled into the casualty department.

Ma Diamond picked up Howl Owl and followed the trolley.

She smiled at the two ambulance men.

"Thank you very much for all your care," she said. "We were so glad to see you."

"I liked the siren in the traffic jam," squeaked Haffertee from the trolley.

"Er ... So did I," said Howl Owl in his very deep voice.

The two men looked at each other and smiled.

Haffertee snuggled up very close to Yo as they were pushed behind some curtains. It was a bit frightening.

Ma sat down beside the trolley and waited.

Then Nurse Pinder came in. She smiled at

Yo and Haffertee.

She began asking Ma Diamond some questions and wrote down the answers in a big folder.

"Doctor is coming to see you soon, Yo," she said.

Just at that moment a man came through the curtains. He was wearing a long white coat and had a thin snake round his neck. Haffertee had seen one of those before. It was really a stethoscope. There was a picture pinned on the top pocket of the doctor's coat. Haffertee could just make out the letters K-I-T-A-K-A.

"Dr Kitaka," said Haffertee, politely. "Good morning."

Dr Kitaka looked at Haffertee and smiled.

"Good morning," he replied. "You must be a detective."

Haffertee thought about that for a moment, looked at Yo and then said, "Yes, I am, especially at Christmas time." (You can read what happened in *Haffertee's First Christmas*.)

Yo chuckled and Ma Diamond smiled.

Howl Owl blinked his big round eyes.

Dr Kitaka frowned. He wasn't sure what to think about that.

Nurse Pinder removed the blanket from Yo.

"Now then, Yo," said the doctor, "let me

have a look at you."

He looked at her very carefully. Then he wrote in the big folder.

"This leg looks a funny shape, Yo," he said. "We shall need some pictures to tell us what has happened to the bones in there, and we will check your elbow at the same time."

He turned to Nurse Pinder and talked quietly for a little while. Then he went out.

Haffertee wondered what was going to happen next.

He didn't have long to wonder.

"We shall have to go to X-ray now," said the nurse. "Would you all like to come?"

Haffertee frowned. He wasn't too sure ab

meeting X Ray. He sounded a bit frightening.

"X Ray," he said, slowly. "Who is he?"

"Not *he*," said Nurse Pinder with a smile. "*It*. The X-ray camera takes pictures of what's inside you. We need to look inside Yo!"

Yo began to sob quietly.

"But you will hurt Yo all over again," said Haffertee. He felt very upset.

Nurse Pinder smiled and stroked his fur.

"No, no, Haffertee," she said. "Just think about it. Does it hurt when you have your picture taken?"

Haffertee shook his head. Pops was always taking photographs of the Diamond family.

"Well, when X-ray takes pictures of your inside, that doesn't hurt either," said Nurse Pinder with a smile.

Yo stopped crying and smiled again.

Haffertee thought about it and nodded slowly.

"Right," he said. "If you say it is all right then I would like to meet Mr X Ray."

Nurse Pinder smiled and turned as a friendly young man opened the curtains.

"Hello," he said. "I'm Andy and I'm going to help nurse."

He pulled the trolley out from behind the curtains.

Yo held Haffertee tight.

Haffertee held Yo tight and could just hear her praying...

"Please God, help me to be brave."

Ma looked round for Howl Owl but couldn't see him anywhere.

She got up and followed Andy and the trolley.

"Wonder what's happened to Howl Owl," thought Haffertee.

But he didn't get an answer.

The journey to X-ray didn't take long.

Suddenly, the sign was there in front of them.

Haffertee saw it first.

X-RAY. A great big sign saying X-RAY, all bright and light.

And there on top of it ... sat Howl Owl.

He was very good at sitting and watching.

Haffertee smiled. His friend was still with him.

That was marvellous!

He breathed a sigh of relief and waited to meet Mr X Ray.

4

Looking into Yo

Haffertee enjoyed being pushed along on a hospital trolley. It was a sort of moving bed.

Yo held Haffertee tightly in her hand.

"Here we are," said Andy, as they went through the swing doors into the X-ray department.

Ma Diamond sat down.

Howl Owl flew over to chat with a big cuddly bear on the table.

"Er... Hello, Teddy Bear," he said.

"Actually," said a very sweet little voice, "my name is Edwina Bear. Hello."

Haffertee and Yo smiled at each other.

Andy, the porter, left. "Byeeeee!" he said happily. "See you!"

"This is Miss Loving," said Nurse Pinder, smiling. "She will look after you now and show you what to do."

"Mr X Ray must be away this week," whispered Haffertee, and Yo struggled to keep in a chuckle. Haffertee *was* funny.

The nurse handed Miss Loving some papers, turned, waved and left.

Miss Loving looked at the papers.

"Good morning, Yo! Good morning, Haffertee!" she said cheerfully, and then pushed the trolley to a high bed in the middle of the next room.

She was very careful as she moved Yo off the trolley and on to the bed.

Yo tried hard to hold back her tears.

Haffertee glared at the lady. She was hurting Yo.

"I'm sorry," said Miss Loving. "I have to have you on this special bed, Yo, for the pictures. Are you comfortable now?"

The pain had gone.

Yo nodded. "Yes," she said, "I'm all right now."

As Yo and Haffertee lay there they could see a large box hanging up over the bed.

They watched as Miss Loving moved it along and round and down until it was just over Yo's bad leg.

"That's the top fixed," she said. "Now for the plate underneath."

Miss Loving slid a big sheet of something very stiff into the special bed frame below Yo's leg.

Then she moved back behind a screen.

"Quite still now, Yo," she said. "Quite still."

Yo stiffened and Haffertee squeezed himself into a ball.

The two of them waited. The picture was going to be taken. There was a click and a whirr and that was all.

Miss Loving came back over to the bed.

"I need to turn you on your side for another picture now, Yo," she said. And she began to move her carefully. Slowly... slowly.

She made sure Yo was comfortable, adjusted everything and then disappeared behind the screen again.

A click and a whirr and that picture was done.

"Now let me see your elbow, Yo."

And the third picture was soon taken.

"That's it, then," said Miss Loving, moving to the door. "You can come and sit in here now, Mrs Diamond, if you like."

Ma Diamond came in with Howl Owl.

She sat down and began to talk to Haffertee and Yo.

Miss Loving went into a small side room to look at the pictures.

"Er... Did it hurt?" asked Howl Owl.

"Not at all," said Yo, with a smile, "Except when I had to move."

"Er... Did it hurt you, Haffertee?" said Howl.

"Not at all," said Haffertee, with his own smile. "Not even when I moved."

They all laughed together.

Miss Loving came back into the room and stood by the bed.

"You did stay very still, Yo," she said, "and all the pictures are good. Will you look after them, please, Mrs Diamond?"

She handed Ma a very big envelope.

"Thank you," said Ma, softly. "Thank you very much."

"It's time for you to go back to the doctor now," said Miss Loving, as she moved Yo across onto the trolley. "I'll just call the porter."

Haffertee, Howl Owl and Yo waited with Ma Diamond for just a few minutes and then Andy appeared.

"Would you like a ride, this time, Howl?" he said.

"Er ... Yes, please," said Howl happily. "Yes, please."

It was great fun riding on the trolley.

Back in the casualty department Andy settled them behind the curtains.

Dr Kitaka came in and Ma handed him the big envelope.

He took the pictures out of the envelope, clipped them in front of a big light and let them all see. Miss Loving had taken a picture of Yo's bones.

Haffertee was very interested to see what Yo looked like inside. "Does everybody have an inside like this?" he asked.

"God made every one of us very carefully," said Dr Kitaka.

He pointed to one of the pictures. "There
are no bones broken in your elbow, Yo, but
these two bones in your leg are fractured. Can
you see how they are broken and crooked?"

Yo said "Yes" and Haffertee and Ma Diamond nodded.

Howl Owl just said "Er...!"

"We shall have to put those two bones back
in line again," said Dr Kitaka gently.

Haffertee gulped.

"Put them straight again?" he whispered.
"Can you really do that?"

"Certainly can," said the doctor. "Then we shall fix a big white plaster cast from your toes to the top of your leg, Yo, to hold the bones straight while they mend."

"Who does the mending then?" asked Haffertee.

Dr Kitaka smiled. "I can put the bones in line again," he said, "But only God can mend them. He is an expert mender."

Haffertee thought about God being an expert mender.

"Bit like Pops Diamond," he muttered, under his breath, and Yo struggled to hold back a laugh.

"But don't worry, Yo," continued Dr Kitaka, "We shall help you go into a very deep sleep so that we can get the bones together without hurting you at all."

Haffertee wondered what would happen to him. But before he could ask, the doctor said, "And Haffertee will be there when you wake up."

"Er . . . Me too," said Howl Owl.

"I'd like that," said Yo quickly. "And you'll be there too, won't you, Ma?"

"Of course," said the doctor, the nurse and Ma Diamond all together.

5

A Log of Wood and a Snowball

Haffertee liked riding with Yo on the hospital trolley. It made him feel very important.

But he was beginning to wonder what would happen next.

They had been to the casualty department. They went to see Mr X Ray, then they went back to the casualty department again.

"We are going to move you to the children's ward now," said Nurse Pinder.

Nurse Pinder and Andy the porter pushed the trolley along the corridor and into a lift. Haffertee was lying on his back like Yo. All they could see was the ceiling.

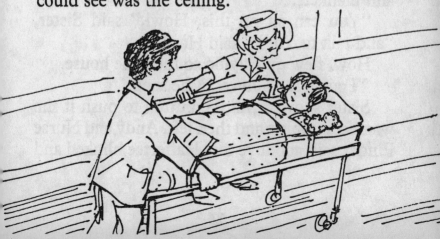

Another nurse called Sister Coidan met them at the door.

"Good morning, Mrs Diamond," she said, "and hello, Yo. We have this side room ready for you."

Haffertee sat up and glanced around.

"There are two beds in here," he said in surprise.

"Oh hello, Haffertee," said Sister. "Nurse Pinder has told me all about you and Howl Owl. I am very pleased to meet you both."

Haffertee bowed slightly. He was pleased to meet the Sister.

"Well," said Sister Coidan, "one bed is for Yo and the other one is for Mrs Diamond."

"Thank you very much," said Ma Diamond.

She was delighted to be able to stay with Yo.

Yo was soon settled on to her bed and Sister and Nurse Pinder made a little house over her leg with a special frame covered by the sheet and blankets.

"You can sit on this, Howl," said Sister, "and talk to Yo."

Howl flew quickly on to the little house.

"Toowit... Toowoo," he sang.

Sister showed Ma the button to push if she wanted anything and then left. Andy and Nurse Pinder said goodbye too. Haffertee blinked and they were gone.

The telephone was brought in and Ma rang Pops.

Then a lady doctor came and listened to Yo's chest and asked Ma some more questions.

"We can only operate if your tummy is empty, Yo," she said.

"Pops wouldn't let me get her some water this morning," said Haffertee rather sadly.

"Good for Pops," said the doctor. "We'll soon get those broken bones sorted out. In a little while Andy will take you to the operating theatre. You'll have a long, deep sleep. And when you wake up your leg will be in plaster. And it won't be long before it's mended."

The doctor smiled and then left.

Haffertee was beginning to feel muddled. All these people!

"I'm a bit scared, Ma," said Yo, when the doctor had gone.

Ma Diamond nodded gently and touched Yo's shoulder.

Yo put her hands up to her face and began to cry.

Ma put a kiss gently on her forehead.

"The Bible says that we can rely on God in all our troubles and pain," she said.

Haffertee sat up quickly on the bed.

"Then we'd better let him know how frightened we are," he said.

Howl Owl blinked, looked at Haffertee and then at Yo. Then he closed his eyes tight.

"Er . . . God," he called. "We're scared."

Ma Diamond took up the conversation.

"Father God, please help the doctor mend Yo's leg," she said.

"You need to get those bones straight, too," said Haffertee.

He felt sure God ought to be told.

Howl Owl nodded.

"Please look after Yo," he hooted.

Yo sniffed a bit and then stopped crying.

"Thank you, God," she said firmly. "I'm not scared any more! I know you are taking care of me."

Yo was quite cheerful as she went into the operating theatre on a trolley. She held Ma's hand and Howl and Haffertee sat close by.

"See you later," said Andy the porter.

"We'll be with you when you wake up," said Ma as Yo floated off into a deep sleep.

After a while Andy and Sister Coidan brought Yo back to the little room where Ma and Haffertee and Howl were waiting. Yo was still very sleepy.

They lifted her gently across to the bed.

Haffertee and Howl watched with pleasure.

Ma Diamond sighed a little.

"Yo will be all right now," said Andy, quietly.

And Haffertee knew he was right.

Long before Yo could open her eyes she felt Ma holding her hand and Haffertee snuggled in against her cheek.

She was content and breathed easily.

Much later than that she did open her eyes.

Haffertee wiggled, Ma squeezed and there was Howl Owl winking at her from on top of the "house".

She managed to say "Hello", before closing her eyes again.

"Are you all right?" asked Haffertee, but Yo didn't hear.

She was asleep again.

The next time Yo opened her eyes she seemed confused.

"Where am I?" she mumbled.

"In hospital with me," said Haffertee, right next to her ear.

"Is it dinner time yet?" asked Yo.

"Er . . . that was ages ago," said Howl.

"Can I see my leg?" said Yo suddenly, not confused any more. "It feels like a log of wood."

"Peep down into the house," said Ma Diamond, lifting the bedding off Yo's tummy.

Yo peered down into the bed, and Haffertee scuttled down inside.

"It looks like a log of wood," he squeaked, "all covered in snow! But it doesn't feel like snow," he added, poking it.

"Out you come, Haffertee," said Ma, making the bed tidy again.

"Does your leg hurt inside the log?" asked Haffertee.

"Not much," said Yo. "But my elbow does."

"That looks like a big snowball," said Haffertee, as Yo lifted her arm out over the sheet.

38

Yo looked at the bandage and touched it gently.

"It feels like soft cotton wool," she said.

For a while no one spoke and Yo dozed off again.

"Can you eat some sandwiches?" said a cheerful-looking nurse, carrying a tray.

Yo was suddenly wide awake.

"Yes, please," she said. "I do feel hungry now."

"Let me sit you comfortably then," said the nurse, helping Yo to sit up.

Yo began to tuck into the sandwiches.

Haffertee sat beside the tray watching.

"Oh—Yo," he kept saying. "Oh—Yo."

Andy had said "Yo will be all right now," and Haffertee could see that he was right. She was.

6

A Long Day

After Yo had eaten the sandwiches, she began to feel much better.

Ma Diamond kept looking at her watch and then at the door.

Haffertee and Howl had a little sleep. All that waiting had made them tired.

Suddenly the door opened slowly and Pops came in, smiling. He gave Yo a long hug.

He held Haffertee in one hand and put his other hand on Howl.

"Sister Coidan tells me that you two have kept Yo very happy," he said. "That's great."

Haffertee looked at Howl and Howl looked at Haffertee. They were glad to be great together.

The next moment Yo's brothers, Chris and Mark, came in. Chris was carrying Mr Jumpastring, Haffertee's wooden friend from the toy cupboard at home. Mr Jumpastring bounced about on a piece of black elastic and sang a lot.

Mark was carrying Rabbearmonklio. He was Haffertee's mixed-up friend. He had the ears of a rabbit, the body of a teddy bear, the face of a monkey and the tail of a lion. He was very gentle and wrote poetry. He was a great smiler and "mmmmmmmed" a lot.

Haffertee was very pleased to see them all. Then big sister Fran came in.

"Da-da-da-dah!" she trumpeted. "How about this?" She was carrying a lovely birthday cake.

Haffertee danced up and down.

"Oh! Oh! Look at the candles," he squealed, as Pops lit them.

It was only yesterday that Haffertee and Yo had watched Ma make the cake. It seemed so long ago now.

Haffertee, Howl Owl, Rabbearmonklio and Mr Jumpastring helped Yo blow out the candles. Then they all sang "Happy Birthday" to her.

Ma Diamond cut the cake and gave everybody a piece. It tasted as good as it looked.

"Right, then," said Pops, when they had finished eating. "Time to go."

"Thank you, God, for all the people who have helped Yo today," he prayed. Everyone said, "Amen."

There were Goodnight kisses and hugs all round and then Fran gave Yo an extra big kiss.

"Grandma sent that," she said.

Yo smiled and gave Fran a big kiss to take back for Grandma, and off they all went, back home to Hillside House.

But not Mr Jumpastring. Ma Diamond fixed him up on the curtain rail and he danced around on his black elastic.

Rabbearmonklio sat close to Howl Owl on the little house over Yo's leg.

Yo was so pleased. Her friends made her feel at home.

But Haffertee was looking very puzzled.

"Why do we always say 'Ah! Men!'," he whispered, "when it is God we are talking to?"

"It's nothing to do with men," said Yo in his ear. "It's just a way of saying 'That goes for me too'."

"Oh!" said Haffertee. "I see."

He smiled and the puzzled look vanished.

They all listened as Ma read a bedtime story.

It had been a long day.

"Goodnight," said Haffertee, with only his head poking out of Yo's pillow case.

"Goodnight!" said the other toys.

Ma Diamond began to sing . . .

> Into dreamland gently now
> You must go.
> Such a lovely place to be
> Don't you know.
> Clouds to make a feathery bed
> Round your head
> Don't you know.
> Dreamland. Dreamland.
> You must go to dreamland.

They were all fast asleep even before she had finished.

Then Ma went to bed. Before long she was asleep too.

She woke up in the night to hear Haffertee whispering.

"Please don't cry, Yo," he said.

Ma looked at her watch in the ward's dim light.

It was just after midnight.

"What's the matter, dear?" she asked, going over to Yo's bed. "Does your elbow hurt?"

"Yes," said Yo, crying gently, "it does, but I keep thinking about my new bike. What will happen to it?"

"Pops will be able to mend it," said Ma. "Don't you worry about it. Your elbow will soon feel much better."

She stroked Yo's head and began to sing about dreamland.

Haffertee settled back in the pillowcase.

Both of them were soon fast asleep again.

Ma Diamond went back to her bed.

It really had been a very long day.

7

The Children's Ward

"Good morning," said the cheerful nurse Yo had met yesterday. She opened the curtains to let the sunshine in. "Here's another lovely day!" she said.

Ma helped Yo to wash and then brushed her hair for her.

They had breakfast together and the nurse came in again.

"Will you come with me for a minute, Haffertee?" she asked. "I need your help."

She picked him up and held him so that he could look at her face. She was smiling.

Haffertee hesitated a moment.

"Um ... Yes, I'll come," he said. So she took him out of the room.

When he came back he was very excited.

"There are seven boys and girls with beds in a big room next door," he said. "Nurse says we can have our bed in there too, Yo. Would you like that?"

Yo thought that that would be a good idea.

"That will be fine," she nodded.

So in no time at all Yo's bed was wheeled along the corridor into the big ward. It was parked between two other beds.

Howl and Rabbearmonklio were sitting on the little house so they had a good ride.

Haffertee sat next to Yo looking very pleased with himself.

Five children were playing in the corner of the big room. They turned to watch as Yo came in. "Hello," they said, rather shyly.

Two other children were still in their beds like Yo. There was a little girl sleeping in one bed. Her father sat by her side.

"Hello, I'm Daniel," said a happy voice from the bed next to Yo. Haffertee had never seen a bed like that before.

"Hello," said Haffertee. "Why has your bed got a climbing frame on it?"

Daniel laughed.

"It isn't a climbing frame. I've broken both my legs and they won't mend properly. I'm on traction."

"Oh," said Haffertee, sounding very wise.

What's he doing on a tractor? he thought to himself.

Before he could ask any other questions a lady called Mrs Walker arrived. She was the physiotherapist. She was going to help Yo to walk.

Mrs Walker started taking away Yo's bedding and the little house. Rabbearmonklio and Howl Owl moved out of her way quickly and watched. Haffertee did the same.

"I've brought these crutches for you," she said. "Just lie straight and I will make them the right size for you. We'll have you up and about in no time."

Very slowly, Yo began to walk with the crutches. The leg in the plaster had to stick out in front.

"That's really very good," said Mrs Walker, smiling.

Haffertee, Howl, Rabbearmonklio and Daniel clapped and cheered.

"Well done, Yo," they said. "Well done."

Dr Kitaka arrived on his rounds and he watched Yo walk a bit more. Mrs Walker helped her back into bed. Yo lifted her plastered leg, and wiggled her toes. The doctor was very pleased with her.

"I'll see you tomorrow morning," he said, "and I'll look at your elbow too. If all is well you can go home at lunchtime.

"Thank you," said Yo, "that'll be great!"

Then the doctor, the physiotherapist, Ma Diamond and Yo turned round and saw Haffertee!

He had fetched two pencils from the play area in the ward and was using them as crutches.

He tried to stick his foot out but he couldn't.

He lost his balance, struggled to hold on to the pencils and then clattered down on the floor.

"Oh, Haffertee," said Mrs Walker, as she picked him up, "I shall have to give you some lessons too."

Sometime later, as he was resting with Yo, and Howl and Rabbearmonklio were back on the little house, Haffertee looked over at Daniel on his tractor.

I wouldn't like to have to stay on my back like that, he thought, and stared up at the curtain rails around the beds.

Suddenly he remembered something.

"Mr Jumpastring," he shouted. "Mr Jumpastring must be still in the little ward."

They gasped. How could they have been so unkind?

"I'll go and fetch him," said Ma, getting up from her chair.

Mr Jumpastring had stopped bouncing on his black elastic. He had been left behind. Forgotten and very sad.

Ma brought him in and fixed him on the curtain rail between Yo and Daniel. Straight away Mr Jumpastring began to bounce and sing and dance.

"Sorry, Mr Jumpastring," said Haffertee. "We shouldn't have left you on your own like that."

Mr Jumpastring smiled and went on bouncing and singing.

"Wheeee! Hooo! Bong!" he bounced. "Wheee! Hooo! Bong!"

Daniel squealed with delight. Lying on his back, he could see Mr Jumpastring easily.

Mr Jumpastring kept on dancing.

Rabbearmonklio was happily humming away in tune with Mr Jumpastring so Haffertee and Howl went for a walk.

They went over into the play area to make a cottage.

That's what Howl called it when he explained it all to Yo.

"Er... We had to stick bits of coloured paper and cloth and pasta onto a big sheet of cardboard," he said. "Er... We were making a picture."

"There was a lady teaching us," said Haffertee. "She said she was so pleased to have a hamster and an owl helping her make her cottage."

Yo burst out laughing. "Not a cottage," she spluttered. "Collage! Collage! We do that at school."

Haffertee and Howl looked at each other in surprise.

Climbing frames, tractors and cottages. Hospital was a real fun place.

Soon after lunch the visitors came with bunches of grapes and flowers, and huge bags of sweets.

Haffertee and Howl and Rabbearmonklio and Mr Jumpastring had a marvellous time. They were offered sweets by nearly everyone.

Pops Diamond arrived with Grandma.

She came in slowly using her stick.

Yo was so glad to see them and she showed them how she could use her crutches.

"You look like a clown on stilts," said Haffertee.

They all laughed together, including Yo.

"Haffertee," she said, as she settled back on her bed, "I do love you."

"Thank you, Yo," he said with a smile. "And I love you too."

Pops and Grandma left soon after that. They wanted to be at home when the others got back from school.

The day ended like the one before. Yo was tired, Haffertee and Howl were tired and Ma Diamond sang a dreamy song.

Mr Jumpastring bounced in time and Rabbearmonklio "Mmmmmmmmmed."

It was time for their Goodnight prayers.

"Thank you, Father God, for all the people who look after us in hospital," said Ma.

"And thank you for taking care of us," said Haffertee.

"Thank you for my friends," said Yo.

Then it was time to sleep.

Yo sighed and tickled Haffertee.

"Hospital isn't so bad after all, is it?" she said softly.

"Not so bad after all at all," he said, chuckling.

Howl Owl blinked and the bright lights went out.

The ward was left in a soft glow.

Ma Diamond went along the corridor to sleep in her own little bedroom. She felt sure that Yo would be able to go home tomorrow.

Ma got into bed. "Thank you, Father God," she said—and fell asleep.

8

Strawberries and a New Mr Jumpastring

The next morning Haffertee woke up to find that Yo was still asleep.

He peeped out of his pillowcase and remembered that he and Yo were in hospital.

Just then Ma Diamond came into the children's ward.

When Yo woke up she helped her to wash herself and then it was breakfast time.

"How is your elbow this morning, Yo?" she asked.

"It doesn't hurt too much," said Yo, "and I didn't wake up in the night."

"I did," said Haffertee. "The little girl in the bed in the corner wasn't very well, so her Daddy came and sat with her."

"Yes, I heard someone come along the corridor to fetch him," said Ma Diamond, remembering the sounds in the night.

"He tells me that Sarah is feeling much better this morning."

They all turned to look at Sarah sitting up eating her breakfast. Her father smiled at them.

Daniel wasn't sitting up for his breakfast. The cheerful nurse was helping him as he lay on his back.

Mr Jumpastring danced and sang for them both . . .

A time to sleep. A time to eat.
A time for Daniel mending.
A time to rest. A time to play.
Just look at how I'm bending!

A time to laugh. A time to cry.
A time for Daniel growing.
A time to sing. A time to dance.
And that's just what I'm doing.

So try to bend and try to sing.
No matter what the weather.
Each day can be a lovely day
As long as we're together.

Daniel smiled and clapped. Mr Jumpastring bowed and bounced.

Daniel's mother was going to have another baby very soon so she couldn't be with him all the time. His father was in the Navy.

Mr Jumpastring had become a real friend.

"What will Daniel do when Mr Jumpastring

comes home with us?" asked Haffertee.

"Er...er... I think he will cry," said Howl Owl slowly.

"Pops told me that he would think of something," said Rabbearmonklio, in his soft hummy voice.

Rabbearmonklio knew a lot about sadness and loneliness because he was all mixed up himself.

Haffertee nodded. Howl Owl nodded. And the three of them agreed that Pops would think of something.

Mrs Walker arrived briskly and said, "Let me see you lift your leg and wiggle your toes, Yo."

Yo lifted her leg and wiggled her toes.

"Now let me see you walking with the crutches."

Yo walked around the ward without letting her plaster touch the floor.

"Wonderful!" said Mrs Walker. "Wonderful!"

Yo got back on the bed with a smile.

The cheerful nurse came next and took off the bandages from around Yo's elbow. Haffertee was rather sad to see the "snowball" disappear.

"Isn't it wonderful, Yo," said the nurse happily. "D'you remember what this elbow looked like two days ago? See how quickly it is healing."

Yo looked and remembered. "Yes," she said quietly.

"God was so clever when he made us," said the nurse. "And he mends us too. See how your skin is healing up!"

"He's a great Maker," thought Haffertee, remembering that he had been made once, too. (You can read about this in *Haffertee Hamster*.) "And God's a great Mender, too."

Yo was looking at her elbow when Dr Kitaka arrived.

He took hold of Yo's arm gently.

"It is looking much better, Yo," he said. "Now, can I see you walk, please?"

He helped Yo off the bed and Ma handed her the crutches.

She set off happily for her walkabout.

"Does that elbow hurt when you put your weight on the crutches, Yo?" asked Dr Kitaka, when she had finished.

"Not much at all," replied Yo.

"Right, then," said the doctor. "Nurse will put a small bandage on it and then..." (He looked at each one of them in turn)... "And then Yo, Haffertee, Howl Owl, Mr Jumpastring, Rabbearmonklio and you, too, Mrs Diamond. You can have your lunch and you can all go home!"

"Thank you, doctor," they said, almost together. "Thank you very much."

Soon after lunch Sister Coidan came in again.

Pops Diamond was with her and he was carrying a plant pot with lots of green leaves and white flowers.

"What on earth is that?" whispered Haffertee to Yo.

She frowned. "No idea," she said at last. "It looks like some sort of plant."

She looked more carefully. "He's dug up a whole strawberry plant," she whispered in surprise.

"I think he will see it nicely here, Mr Diamond," said Sister, as Pops stood the pot on Daniel's locker.

"What is it?" asked Daniel.

"In a week or two these flowers will turn into strawberries," explained Pops. "Ask nurse to water the plant each day and then you can eat your own strawberries."

"Honest?" asked Daniel.

"Wait and see," said Pops. "We will come and see, too."

Then Andy the porter appeared pushing a wheelchair.

Daniel began to cry.

"Are you *all* going now?" he sobbed.

Yo swallowed hard. Haffertee could guess what was coming.

"Is Mr Jumpastring going with you?" asked Daniel softly.

Howl Owl closed his eyes.

Mr Jumpastring stopped dancing.

Rabbearmonklio sniffed and Ma Diamond looked at the floor.

With a twinkle in his eye, Pops put his hand into his pocket.

"Chris made this for you last night, Daniel," he said happily.

And out of his pocket he took a new Mr Jumpastring.

"This one is for you," said Pops, "with our love."

Daniel gasped. Ma Diamond caught her breath.

"Wonderful," she said.

"Oh! Thank you!" said Daniel.

Everyone felt very happy. Haffertee was so excited he nearly fell off the bed.

"Come up here," sang old Mr Jumpastring, dancing again.

So Pops tied the new little wooden man on the curtain rail.

He soon learned Daniel's song.

The two of them danced and sang and bounced together on their black elastic.

"I'm happy now," said Mr Jumpastring.

Pops took him down from the rail.

"Goodbye, Daniel. Please talk to your new friend so that he won't feel strange when we've gone."

Daniel smiled and watched and smiled and thanked. Then he waved them all "Goodbye!"

Andy helped Yo to get into the wheelchair. She felt very special being wheeled along the corridors, into a lift and then out on to the car park.

Howl Owl and Rabbearmonklio sat on her lap.

Haffertee was in one hand and Mr Jumpastring in the other. He wasn't forgotten this time.

Pops helped Yo into the back of the car.

The rest of them piled in.

"You drive, Ma," said Pops as he got into the passenger seat.

Andy waved as they drove away.

"We're on our way again," sighed Haffertee. "On our way home."

Pops Diamond turned to smile at Ma.

"It'll be nice to have you home," he said.

Haffertee just couldn't wait to get home, and before long, there they were.

9

Home on the Rocker

When the Diamond family arrived home from
the hospital Grandma was sitting in her chair by
the window, waiting for them.

She smiled when she saw the car turning the
corner.

Yo waved merrily to her as they drew up in
front of the house.

"I'll carry you up the steps," said Pops.
"You mustn't try those on your own yet."

Ma Diamond gave Yo her crutches as they came into the house and Yo walked into the lounge.

"It's lovely to see you home again," said Grandma, looking over her glasses. "Lovely to see all of you."

Haffertee nodded. Rabbearmonklio hummed. Mr Jumpastring bounced and Howl Owl blinked.

They were all glad to see Grandma again, too.

Yo settled carefully on the settee. The doctor had told her she would have to rest her leg and put it up when she wasn't walking.

"We have been praying for you so much, Yo," said Grandma.

Haffertee thought about all that prayer and wondered how God managed with so many people talking at once. He didn't wonder for long. He felt sure God could handle it.

Howl fluttered over to sit on the arm of Grandma's chair.

Haffertee looked round the room.

"Oh, isn't it small?" he said at last.

Ma Diamond smiled. "Yes," she said, "it does seem small after the big ward in the hospital."

Suddenly the back door opened and in burst

Fran and Chris. Mark wasn't far behind.

"Hello, Yo," spluttered Chris. "How was the new Mr Jumpastring?"

"Daniel loved him," she said, all smiles.

"Hello, Yo," puffed Mark. "How's your plaster?"

Yo nodded towards her leg and Mark looked at it carefully.

"I've got to take it back again soon, to have a rocker fitted so that I can put some weight on my foot," she said.

Dr Kitaka had explained all that to her.

Haffertee nodded. "If she falls over then, she will be off her rocker," he said, chuckling.

Grandma smiled. "Don't be such a tease, Haffertee," she said.

"Would you like to play Snakes and Ladders, Yo?" said Fran, suddenly. "Grandma and I had a great game last night."

"No! No!" said Mark. "Television first.'

It was good to be home again.

Ma got tea ready while they watched television.

After tea, Pops and Fran did the washing up.

"Now," said Grandma, "now for the great signing ceremony. Bring on the plaster!"

Yo wondered what on earth was going to happen.

"Please, Yo," said Fran. "Can we draw on your plaster?"

"Oh yes," said Yo.

Pops lifted her carefully up on to the big kitchen table.

And everybody drew something on her plaster ... something about her hospital trip.

Grandma drew some crutches.

Pops drew a bike.

Ma drew an ambulance.

Fran drew a birthday cake.

Chris drew the second Mr Jumpastring.

The first Mr Jumpastring drew Daniel in his climbing frame.

Mark drew a patched up Haffertee on a hospital bed, and Haffertee drew Yo's broken leg mended.

Howl Owl drew the X-ray sign, and Rabbearmonklio drew the strawberry plant.

Yo's plaster began to look like rainbows in a muddle.

It was a wonderful sight.

Then it was bedtime and Yo was so pleased to be back in her own bed again. Haffertee snuggled inside the pillowcase and Howl Owl sat watching from his usual place on the shelf above the door.

But just as they were getting settled, Frank the Tank began gurgling and singing and

burbling in the airing cupboard. (You can read about Frank the Tank in *Haffertee's New House.*)

The cupboard next to it opened and out came Rabbearmonklio followed by all the toys dancing and singing.

Everyone here is happy again
Yolanda is back in her bed.
Home from the hospital happy again
Yolanda is back in her bed.

It was a lovely song and a wonderful sight.
Howl and Haffertee joined in loudly.

"That was even better than the practice," puffed Haffertee when the singing and dancing was over.

Yo smiled. "Would you like to draw on my plaster, too?" she asked.

They would and they did . . . all of them. In no time at all, the plaster was completely covered.

"Thank you very much," said Yo when they had finished. "It really is wonderful to be home again. And I am very sleepy."

She yawned and off she went into dreamland and her friends came too.

The next few days went by rather slowly.

Yo and Grandma did all sorts of jigsaws and played all sorts of games.

Haffertee made sure that Yo did her exercises. He took her for walks round the house and in the garden.

Fran taught her how to use water-colour paints.

Chris and Mark showed her how to watch television!

But at last it was time to go back to the hospital.

Ma Diamond took Yo to the Outpatients Department and Nurse Pinder gasped when she saw all the drawings and colours on her plaster.

"Who on earth did all that?" she asked, smiling.

"The family and the toys in the toy cupboard," said Yo.

"That is a pretty picture," said Nurse Pinder. "Like twenty rainbows rolled into one."

Haffertee smiled. He wondered what twenty rainbows rolled into one would look like.

Dr Kitaka was very pleased with Yo and Nurse Pinder arranged for a rocker to be added to the foot of Yo's plaster.

Mrs Walker came to see how it looked.

"It will be really dry by tomorrow," she said. "Then you can put just a little weight on it each time the two crutches go down."

Yo smiled.

"Can I go to school tomorrow, then?" she asked excitedly.

"Not tomorrow, Yo," said Mrs Walker. "Just have a day or two at home practising and then you can go if you like."

Yo nodded and looked at the rocker.

There was some nice new clean plaster round her ankle and foot.

"Now my friends at school can sign it as well," she said.

And they did! They wrote their names and drew pictures.

They were so pleased to see Yo back.

Yo enjoyed showing them how to walk on crutches with a rocker and the teachers and the children were very thoughtful about chairs in the playground and being careful when Yo was walking along the corridors.

Haffertee had a great time talking about ambulance rides, trolley rides, wheelchair rides, X-ray pictures and tractors and cottages and climbing frames. He was glad to be back at school too.

10

Off with the Plaster

"Will they use a hammer and chisel?" asked Haffertee.

"Whatever for?" said Grandma.

"To get Yo's log off," he said.

"Haffertee," said Grandma, "You know they won't do that."

"It's hard enough," said Haffertee, poking at Yo's multi- coloured plaster. "What will they do with it when it comes off?"

He was thinking it would make a good garden house for him if Yo took her foot out.

"It'll be a bit of a mess, I think," said Ma Diamond.

Yo looked at the lovely pictures and shapes and colours. It made her think of all her friends.

"Come along then, Yo," called Ma, interrupting her dreaming. "Time to go. Say goodbye to Grandma."

Haffertee turned and ran to the bottom stair.

"It's time to go to the hospital," he shouted

up the stairs to Howl, Rabbearmonklio and Mr Jumpastring. "Time to see Yo's plaster for the last time. Time for Mr X Ray to take his last picture of Yo."

He made it sound like a great adventure.

Ma shushed at him and hustled them all out to the car.

They were just shutting the car doors when Pops arrived from the garden with a small basket of strawberries and a huge bunch of roses.

"Give the strawberries to Daniel, please," he said. "The flowers are for everybody. Ask Sister Coidan to spread them around."

So off they went to the Outpatients Department of the hospital once again.

"What a lot of people and plasters and sticks and crutches," said Haffertee, as they sat down to wait.

At last it was their turn.

"Mrs Diamond," said a voice.

Ma got up quickly. "Can you bring Yo in here, please?" said a nurse.

Haffertee, Howl Owl, Rabbearmonklio and Mr Jumpastring followed Yo into the next room and climbed up on to her bed.

They watched with their mouths open as the nurse cut off the plaster. She had a special saw, a bit like Pops' electric drill.

"It makes a loud, loud noise," she said. "But it doesn't hurt at all."

Yo was a bit disappointed to see all the pictures and colours and shapes breaking up, but she soon got over that.

"Your skin is all flaky," said Haffertee in surprise.

"It has been shut up in the dark for so long without a wash," said the nurse, smiling. "I'm sure you'll want to get into the bath when you get home," she said. "Warm water will do it good."

The nurse turned towards the door as Andy came in with the wheelchair.

"Now for the X-ray," she said.

Miss Loving in the X-ray department seemed pleased to see them all. She took the pictures quickly and when they were ready Andy carried them and his passengers back to the Outpatients Department. They sat down and waited once more.

"In here now, please," said Dr Kitaka.

And in they went.

"Hello," he said. "Now let's see these bones."

He clipped the X-rays in front of the special light.

"Hmmmmmm. They are not broken and bent now, Yo. Look."

They all looked.

"They look swollen and fat," said Haffertee.

Dr Kitaka smiled. "When God mends something," he said, "he makes a good job of it. The body grows some extra bone to make sure it is strong. Now, Yo, let me see you bend your knee and move your foot up and down . . . now round and round. How does that feel?"

"It won't work properly," said Yo, trying hard not to cry.

"Does it hurt?" asked Haffertee.

"No," sobbed Yo, "but I can't make it move."

Ma was upset too.

"This is quite normal," said the doctor gently. "In a week's time you'll be running around with no problem."

"I see you've brought her other sock and shoe, Mrs Diamond. Good. Please put them on for her."

He waited while Ma put them on Yo's foot. Then he said, "Now show me how you stand up, Yo."

Yo stood up slowly and moved around.

She began to feel much happier.

The leg felt very funny but it was walking her about.

Mrs Walker showed Yo some new exercises and that was that.

"Can we go to see Daniel now?" asked Mr Jumpastring.

Ma nodded and off they went.

Daniel was still lying on his back but he was singing away merrily as his own Mr Daniel Jumpastring danced and bounced and sang.

Yo's Mr Jumpastring nodded and smiled.

"Hello," said Yo. "How are you this morning?"

"Fine," said Daniel. "Fine. Guess what?

Doctor says I can get off this bed tomorrow."

"That *is* good news," said Ma.

"I'm so pleased," said Yo, and Haffertee nodded.

"And I've eaten all my strawberries," said Daniel. "They were lovely."

"Aha!" said Yo mysteriously. "Look what we've got." And she brought the little basket of strawberries out from behind her back.

Daniel reached for one and popped it in his mouth.

"Umm!" he said with a smile. "Lovely. Lovely... but not as nice as mine!"

They talked for a little while and then Ma said it was time to go back to Hillside House.

As soon as she got home Yo soaked her itchy skin in a lovely warm bath. The exercises were easier already.

And then what a celebration they had.

Grandma and Yo helped Ma make fruit salad and jellies and sandwiches.

Fran and Ma had baked lots of cakes last evening.

Pops was looking after the fizzy drinks, ice-cream, sweets and crisps—all the treats that were saved for parties.

It was a real feast.

Fran and Chris and Mark set up a table with a colourful paper table cloth in the garden.

"I tried to make the cloth look like your

plaster, Yo," said Chris.

Yo's birthday bicycle stood there all mended and painted just waiting for her to ride when she was properly fit again.

Some of Yo's friends from school and all the toys from the toy cupboard came.

Mr Jumpastring sang Daniel's song and Rabbearmonklio read one of his own poems.

> When your bike has hit the ground
> And your leg is broken down
> An ambulance takes you to town
> Think of all your friends.
>
> If you're feeling all alone
> Your leg is heavy like a stone
> All you want to do is moan
> Think of all your friends.
>
> And here we are Yo, everyone
> All so pleased to see you home
> Glad that God has fixed the bone
> We are all your friends.

Howl Owl sat on the fence watching and blinking.

"All hands to the clearing up now," shouted Pops when the visitors had gone. "It won't take us long." And it didn't.

"Bedtime then," said Ma. "Go carefully up

the stairs, Yo."

So she did. Having two proper legs made it easier.

Yo undressed slowly, put on her nightie and then climbed into her very own bed in her very own room.

Haffertee snuggled into the pillowcase.

Howl Owl settled on the shelf above the door.

They were waiting for Ma Diamond to come to read to them.

But on this very special night the whole Diamond family came.

Pops read a story from the Bible about Jesus healing people with bad legs so that they could walk again.

"Thank you, God, for the hospital," he said, "and everybody there who helps you do your work. You've mended Yo's leg and we know that you will make it strong again."

"And please make Daniel well soon," sighed Yo.

The whole family said "Amen" ... except Haffertee.

"That goes for me too," he squeaked.

Also from Lion Publishing

THE HAFFERTEE STORIES

Janet and John Perkins

Haffertee is a soft-toy hamster. Ma Diamond made him for her
little girl, Yolanda (usually known as Diamond Yo), when her real
pet hamster died.

These books tell the adventures of the inquisitive, amusing and
lovable Haffertee Hamster—at home, at school and in the world
outside.

There are eight Haffertee books in the series. Illustrated with
line drawings, each contains ten short stories, ideal for bedtime
reading or reading aloud.

HAFFERTEE HAMSTER
ISBN 0 7459 2067 5

HAFFERTEE'S NEW HOUSE
ISBN 0 7459 2068 3

HAFFERTEE GOES EXPLORING
ISBN 0 7459 2069 1

HAFFERTEE'S FIRST CHRISTMAS
ISBN 0 7459 2070 5

HAFFERTEE GOES TO SCHOOL
ISBN 0 7459 2017 3

HAFFERTEE'S FIRST EASTER
ISBN 0 7459 2072 1

HAFFERTEE GOES ON HOLIDAY
ISBN 0 7459 2400 X

HAFFERTEE GOES TO HOSPITAL
ISBN 0 7459 2401 8

More stories for younger readers from LION PUBLISHING: